BUL

A Narcissistic Control Freak from Womb to Tomb

Jack Mason

Published in July 2022 by emp3books Ltd
6 Silvester Way, Church Crookham, Fleet, GU52 0TD

©Jack Mason 2022

ISBN: 9781910734483

www.emp3books.com

CONTENTS

THE EULOGY

I have the need to explain what I did and why I am not a bad man for doing it. I needed to sanitise myself and others after the hurt that my sibling caused for so many people throughout his whole life.

What follows is brief. Only good people deserve long stories to be told about them. Billy was so evil that he deserved nothing longer than what I said at his funeral.

It all began by me attempting to write a eulogy for my brother. It was short, and I would like to say, sweet. However, although it was brief, I told the truth, and it was bitter. My words were as follow:

"Billy Mason was a bullying scumbag and narcissist who died with lots of money in the bank but without a single friend in the world. I am only here because I promised that he would be buried after his death."

The undertaker gasped as I walked away to the fresh air outside.

THE WOMB

I ask myself if it was nature or nurture. For him, I am sure, it was both.

Maybe because his parents had both grown up during the Second World War and his mother had developed an admiration for the armed forces, William and Margaret got together. He was in the navy and his motivation in life was the expression of his masculinity through lust, and for her she wanted to fall in love with a hero. They were opposites but having got her pregnant he did what was expected in those days and married our mother out of obligation. After the reality of marriage sank in, he developed a love for alcohol instead of her. He had been handsome and of good height, mother said, but after the ravages of alcohol and idleness took their toll, I remember him as a man with a strained face and whose crumbling body stumbled around.

My Brother, Billy Mason, was born on the 4th of April 1958 and died sixty-four years later, almost to the day. He was named William, after his father, but was known as Billy-the-Kid by the family to give him his own identity.

A lot of information was given to me by his mother or, in fact, our mother when I was about to become a father for the first time.

She told me that even in the womb Billy was a bully. Yes, he was a little shit even before he was born and remained that way and as he grew he became an even bigger shit. While mother was carrying this monstrous embryo, he was developing his skills at hurting.

Maybe because his father's sperm was damaged by the nuclear tests he witnessed on the Christmas Islands or from the vast amounts of alcohol he drank, something caused his child to be born a horror.

In actual fact, Billy had three fathers. One was the quiet sullen and self pitying one when he had a hangover. The second was the man who enjoyed sitting in the garden come rain or shine, chatting with his imaginary friends while they were apparently sharing copious amounts of scrumpy, a strong cider, and having a

3

whale of a time. The third was the argumentative and violent one who would lash out with evil words, accusations and his fists when he felt he had been taken for a fool, which he was.

Because of the way father was, our family needed money and the local grocer, Mr George, offered mother a job in which she found comfort and a safe haven away from our little council house in a run-down area of a small town in Dorset. That was better than the alternative, a high-rise apartment block in an inner city where the only greenery to see was the mould that grew on the wet and soiled ceiling.

For William, the alcohol caused erectile disfunction and he lost the ability to have sex. I purposefully missed out saying, making love, because he never knew that screwing a woman and making love were two totally different things.

She also told me that when she was carrying Billy, he kicked so hard that it hurt her badly. As if sensing her pain with his embryonic brain, it made him kick again and again, harder and harder as if to signify his ability to cause distress to somebody bigger than himself even though that person was sustaining his life.

Therefore, the question as whether or not his evil controlling and sadistic streak came from nature or nurture is simple. As I said before, I think it came from both.

As father was a jealous man, he accused mother of being a whore. He was even suspicious of people who were out of reach. Apparently, mother had wanted to name me James, after the actor but because James Mason was a handsome man with a smooth voice that was like the purring of a Rolls Royce, William insisted that I should be called Jack, after his father.

During the birth of Billy, mother screamed out loud in agony, distress and hurt. She continued her cries of pain for many years after the delivery of her baby from hell. The hurt was far more severe than the slaps, punches and broken limbs given to her by her husband that would subside over time when he got weaker up until the point when he died in pain, as if karma had taken its revenge.

4

GROWING UP

As I have said, father was a drunk and taught Billy that an argument, a threat and a fist would subdue mother. 'Stand up for yourself, son. Don't let nobody stand in your way.'

The blueprint for the rest of his life was created. He knew what it was like to be hurt for not abiding by his father's rules and practiced his methods on me and our sister Sally. Using threats and punches, he made us do the chores that he had been given so he could watch in comfort during the times father was in his alcohol fuelled world while mother was working in her safe haven of Mr George's grocery shop.

He never praised us for doing well but instead he hit us if we were not perfect, and to his mind, we never were. He enjoyed the power he had over us.

He insisted that mother would buy him smart clothes that would impress others and give the impression that he came from a family that was 'well-off'. He was about the same height and build as his peers but he puffed himself up to pretend that he was bigger. He slicked his dark brown hair down. The Brylcreem boys, the wartime fighter pilots he saw in the films he watched always had good looks and attracted admiration. They also had the added bonus of showing menace when they were in combat.

The only benefit that I got from him was that his hand-me-down shirts, jumpers and trousers were still smart even though showing signs that they were close to being worn out. That ended when I outgrew him. That is when he stopped bullying me.

At school, Billy tried to make his mark and acted the strong man. As a result, the other children called him Silly Billy and after a while he reacted with his fists to stop them. The playground became his battleground.

'I'm not a bully I am Billy. I hate nicknames', he said to the people who behind his back called him Billy the Bully before he found out.

Billy broke toys and if he couldn't keep them he hurt the person to whom they belonged.

That malevolent guidance given to him by father was hard-wired into his mind. He knew from the hot-blooded approach to life that bullying was the best tactic for getting what he wanted. He terrorised other children into pretending that they liked him, or else.

He built a gang around him and he would reward them by not hurting them and by sharing his stolen sweets shoplifted with skill to keep them loyal to his cause which was, of course, himself.

He never had real friends. He thought having people who knew him well was a liability. I know that friends are people you can rely on and they can rely on you. He refused to have any faith in the well meaning of other people unless he was manipulating them. He saw friends as a weakness. Yet he called people buddies or mates as a method to make them submit to him. He gave a bit of money here and a favour there and they were hooked.

Throughout the rest of his life, self-doubt was his big issue. It was like a monstrous zit that, no matter how hard he squeezed, it just remained and became larger and more fixed on his forehead.

TEENAGE YEARS

In the first year of senior school, Billy found that he was the youngest and least grown of the other boys. He realised that a big number of smaller boys had an advantage over a lesser number of the bigger kids. Blood on others was a medal. Blood on himself was a motivation for revenge. They would have to lose much more than he did.

At this new school he needed a different gang and recruited them in the way he did before, sweets, but cigarettes were added to his list. As the boys who were older were full of testosterone from puberty, the best tactic was to show numbers who would potentially be a force rather than going for direct conflict.

He watched the older lads and got to know their strengths and weaknesses and built his own learning curve that would be useful when he became an adult.

Admired by his cohort of young gladiators, he knew that what he had always wanted was attention. It had to be positive or else he would do something that got him negative reactions.

Our mother, when I was in my teenage years, told me some interesting things. The most important thing for me was that William was in fact, not my father. She explained how it had come about and in tears, she sobbed out her story. My real dad was the man who ran the local grocery shop and who employed mum after William was incapable of working anywhere.

The widower, Mr George liked mother and they shared a love life that William was unable to have. Mother told me that our younger sister, Sally, was also a product of Mr George. It explained why Sally and I had blond hair and blue eyes whilst Billy had brown hair and brown eyes.

I was glad when mum, told me that I did not share Billy's father in my genes. It explained why our sibling rivalry was more extreme than with others.

For me, genetics played a huge part in my own protection. Luckily, Mr George was a big and strong man and I had inherited his build. By the time Billy was thirteen, I was bigger and stronger than him and the two-year age gap disappeared. If he hit me, I would hit him back harder and he stopped bullying me and saved his anger to take out on others who could not defend themselves. As much as he enjoyed inflicting physical and emotional pain, he could not take being hurt back.

The thankful thing was that Billy had not turned to drink as his father had and so stopped the need to shout spiteful and cruel words at mother. He had come to appreciate that women are an important part of a man's happiness and spent time getting to know and understand girls at school.

Even after a few years, he still had no idea.

When he was old enough, he got himself a Saturday job at one of Mr George's competitor's shops as mother told him to stay away from where she worked.

He stacked shelves, flattened boxes and wired the cardboard into bundles for the company that took them away to be reused. He stole what he could, not because he wanted the items, but it felt as if he was using resources of others to please himself. He tried his hand at selling in the shop and would smarten up for work.

Phyllis was a regular customer who found Billy attractive even at his young age of fifteen. She liked to use her looks and build to control men. One Saturday, just before closing, she walked, or stumbled in truth, into the shop and told Billy to meet her when he finished. She would be waiting across the road in the phone box. She had been drinking through the day and felt bored and in need of some fun.

Billy checked his hair and tie were straight, washed his hands and walked over to the place he had been told to meet the woman who had told him to do so.

Without wondering why he was following her directions and guided by the streetlights on that mild October evening, he crossed the road and got into the phone booth. He looked around as if she could be hiding in such a small place. He heard a knock on the glass and a finger beckoned him to come out and join her.

Phyllis grabbed his hand and marched away, pulling him as

she went as his mother had when he was a toddler. Billy had admired her when she did her bits of shopping before. About twenty, her pretty face, slim figure and bleached blond hair had caught the attention of many men but to be grabbed out of the blue, the young Billy was feeling out of his depth as he had with the girls at school. Men could be handled with a threat or punch, but girls and women were an alien race.

More confusing was, after their arrival in the park and under the cover of the shrubs she, in one movement, put one hand down the front of his trousers while the other hand grabbed his and thrust it up her skirt.

Billy had no idea what to do next. His knowledge of a woman's anatomy had come from watching Sally in the bathroom through the keyhole.

Leaning against a tree, she slid his trousers and pants down, then her panties and guided him into her. After a few seconds it was over and he was confused but happy that he had lost his virginity. Phyllis laughed. 'That was quick. We will need to do it again young man. Hey, I don't even know your name, mine is Phyllis by the way. I liked you because you were always charming in the shop and I needed somebody who would enjoy sex for the sense of pleasure rather than being used by older men who treat females as a commodity for use before throwing them away.'

Billy knew that already. Every time she had come into the shop, somebody would notice her and say out loud that Phyllis had been looking for something that would make her happy that was not on sale.

The following Monday morning, his English teacher mentioned that he had seen Billy with a woman who looked old enough to be his mother. Billy told him it had been his auntie Bridget who wanted to buy him some fish and chips. The subject was dropped even though the teacher had a puzzled look on his face.

That was the start of a series of training sessions when she would tell him what to do to be a better lover. He learnt fast enough to know most of the tricks he needed to have up his sleeve before Phyllis told him that it would have to end.

9

Billy did not want that to happen and told her that he was only fifteen and she had had sex with an underage boy. She had even been seen by one of his teachers. On the strength of his coercion, they carried on having occasional routine sex until Billy got bored and ended it. It had to be done that way, on his terms, not hers.

He had learnt more about the use of threat to control and how to use women. They like being charmed and feeling as if they are treasured rather than just objects to give short term pleasure. From now on he knew the lies to tell to get his short-term desires.

His approach to the girls at school changed. 'Hey,' he thought, 'if I can charm the pants off a twenty-year-old stunner, then I can have my way with these girls with no experience.' Including himself, they were all sixteen and it was now legal to have sexual relationships even if the girls were tricked into it by threat and/or by flattery.

Up until the time he left school at eighteen he seduced many girls and raped others who rejected his advances but blackmailed them into silence afterwards.

The amateur now had become the professional abuser.

FORGING HIS LIFE

Billy knew that education was the key to making money. Through lack of interest in studying, he had failed his 'A' levels and went to work in a bank as an office boy at first and then was promoted to a junior clerk.

He knew that dressing to play the part he wanted rather than the one he had was a key to success. He bought clothes that made him seem to strangers that he was, in fact, the bank manager.

After a few years he joined a big insurance company with his fake degree in business and economics. He was lucky in-so-much as there was no Internet with which to check information.

Billy's degree came easily. While he was working in the bank there was a rumour that one of the customers, a professor at the local university was a homosexual. These were the days when being gay was still a crime.

Billy knew his home address from his bank account details and he would follow him and soon realised that there was one public toilet this man visited fairly frequently. Either he had a weak bladder or there was another purpose. Billy would follow him in and pretend to be having a pee while the professor disappeared into a booth as if he was going to have a shit. Then another man appeared and went into the same booth. Billy then had the method to gain a degree without working for it.

One day he went to the man's house and stated in very simple terms that unless the professor gave Billy a letter on university headed note paper, then his career would be ended.

It needed to say that he was an exemplary pupil and had worked hard to gain his first-class degree in business and economics, the professor's speciality. Once received, he promised that he would destroy the evidence he had against him.

He reminded him that if any company asked for confirmation of what was in the letter and the Professor gave a negative reply, then Billy would resurrect the information he had against him and make it public. When the vulnerable are threatened then they are too weak to ask for proof. In fact, Billy had none.

11

I have withheld the name of the university and the professor because I consider them to be victims.

The letter was as follows:

"To whom it may concern, William Mason was a perfect student, very knowledgeable and his ability to learn was exemplary. He was an example to everybody and I wish him well in whatever career he chooses and I am sure that he will make a perfect employee."

Billy started work with no knowledge of the insurance business or how corporations work, but he had a vast encyclopaedia of knowledge about using people for his gain.

He knew that you could control others by threats to their security as well as by physical hurt. Everybody likes to be built up by promises and charm.

His peers at school had either gone off to work or had gone to university. For the next three years his life would be sitting behind a desk doing boring things, talking to people on the phone and honing his skills of control and exploitation to the maximum so when he graduated from the University of Billy, rather than climbing the business career ladder, he would take the express elevator.

One important lesson he learnt from his father was that drink was a friend and enemy, one disguised as the other. He would go for after work drinks with his colleagues of equal status, or even better, seniors and have a nice time.

That would be repeated a few times until the time was right to spike drinks with vodka or whatever else would work to get them drunk enough to make mistakes. The method he liked was ordering doubles for others and singles for himself.

Sometimes they would confide delicate business or personal information that Billy stored in his mind ready to use at the proper time for his own benefit.

He decided that working for a company should really be working for himself. He needed to gain what he wanted and that was a mix of money, sex and acclaim.

He had the ability to dream big. He knew where he wanted to go on the career ladder and spent his first income on buying clothes that made him look like the boss. If he dressed like a winner then that is what he would become. His promotions came fast and he had a team of people who would be able to help him to keep on moving upwards.

Being like a chameleon and being able to change his outward character at will, he used an acronym that was ABC,DEF.

If people were senior to him, 'if Above then Be Charming'. If they were junior then 'if Down then Establish Fear'.

Simple, but he thought it was effective in reaching his goals. He knew that people in work worry about their job security and he could use that as a weapon.

Looking back, his style was similar to the Gunnery Sergeant Hartman in Full Metal Jacket before the film was made. He used put-downs and insults to create fear but he was more subtle because he was in a business that was different to the army. He believed in gain through pain, but the hurt was always felt by others.

He chose his employees, but having an inbuilt distrust of them, once they had served their purpose or had lost his confidence in being able to help satisfy his needs, he removed them in the same way that a gardener dead-headed roses once their attraction had faded and were no longer able to please.

Always a narcissist, he loved himself and his abilities to succeed in all things. He, in his mind, was the best and most certainly better than those who ranked above him at the time. He spent hours in front of the mirror grooming himself and worked his charm to make sure he appeared in every PR photo that bragged about achievement. At one point he grew a moustache and trimmed it to look smart. After a while he thought of his father with his smoke and beer stained facial hair and shaved it off.

He had a simple strategy. Reduce costs to boost the profit ratios and the easiest way to do that was to reduce staff expenditure on wages. He removed any handsome men who he felt threatened his standing with the women. Women were great because they were cheaper than men and could give equal, if not better, results. Besides, they were more interesting to socialise with and to use if they were willing to give him what he wanted for their security and more money, he thought.

As a reminder of his use of charm and promises, he kept Venus Fly Trap plants in his office, his joke for himself. They would not last long unless the windows were opened , to let flies in so in time they were given to his juniors to look after. He would demand that windows were opened on warm days without giving the real reason. If the plants died then he would berate them in public about the idea that if they could not look after flowers, how could they nurture the customers.

He knew that carnivorous plants attracted what they needed by offering sweet nectar and when the triggers were touched, the flying insects were held by the closing flaps to enable them to be digested. 'What a great way to get what you want. Attract, trap and consume.'

For Billy, charm, flattery and empty promises were his nectar used in his manipulative armoury. Of course, the corpses had to be disposed of with good severance pay and references once used to build his ego and fulfil his sexual needs. He was an expert in putting the offensive into 'charm offensive'.

The women he used were chosen for the one objective. To satisfy him. They needed to be able to work efficiently but he would look at their CVs and application forms to spot his targets.

He would note their pastimes and hobbies and file it away for later use. They had to be attractive and if everything fitted together, they would be employed.

He worked on his plans to grow the business and thereby his rewards.

He would bully people into buying insurance, death plans, by making people feel guilty for not having them. His first line would be 'when my grand father died the family could not afford a proper funeral and everybody hated him and his memory because he had been selfish enough not to pay for his own funeral'.

By buying into a life insurance plan it meant the people would love the victim during their life as well as after their death. It was his technique for pushing people into paying out money that they didn't have as a guarantee that they would continue to be loved.

He had other plans. He checked out people with potentially high pay-outs on death. He then looked for those who had aged next of kin and who were in a position to receive money with no plans for leaving it to anybody other than charities. He found a suitable target, Mr and Mrs Hardy. He met up with the couple and advised them to invest their money in housing that would bring in rental income which would then be given to their chosen charities. He would be the man to arrange that and 'for tax purposes' the money should go to him as the trustee. They could also sign over their house to ensure that the money was well spent. He needed to wait until the death of one of the couple before he got his hands on their funds, but it would become worthwhile after just a few years.

What Billy wanted was ownership. Not happy to share, he wanted to take over the company and thereby stop any attempts to get rid of him. He knew that the world was against him and worried that even being the CEO would subject him to the scrutiny of a board of directors and shareholders. However, he knew the company was too big for him to own it lock stock and barrel.

A year after his deal with Mr and Mrs Hardy, they died suddenly with just a month between their passing. Billy read about what had happened, rubbed his hands together and spoke to the solicitor about getting the house. When he was told that they had changed their wills and that all the money from the sale of the house and their savings had been donated to a charity for the welfare of donkeys, he became so angry that he threw his phone against a wall where it smashed into small pieces.

He needed a different plan to make money. He decided to bounce the share price by making allies of financial journalists while keeping his identity secret.

He used the information that had been leaked from drunken mouths and would give negative information to lower the value of the company and then buy shares.

After a while he would leak positive information and sell them at a good profit. He knew what he was doing was illegal but he covered his tracks well.

He made enough money during the few years that he managed to get away with it and invested his money in a property which he rented out. He had enough left over to pay for the deposit on a grand apartment that would give him privacy being on the seventh floor where no passers by could look in.

RELATIONSHIPS

He would rent his house to single women and then he offered an armistice against the rise of rentals by offering his special deal of payment with cash or flesh. He wanted to own the inhabitants as well as the house. After a while, when he got bored with the occupants, he would evict them and select a new woman.

He discovered that lonely, vulnerable and unattached women were the lucrative resource he was looking for. He would get into their minds with a light touch on the arm and then the neck, always moving away to prove that he was after nothing from them. It was a better ice breaker than a few gin and tonics. It worked faster and cost him nothing. If they enjoyed the attention then they needed to move towards him to get more.

He read numerous books on body language and used his knowledge for gain from his work and from the women he wanted. He knew that mirroring another person's position and look endeared them to him. It was another language for being soul mates and pulled them in.

And in conversations, he always liked what they liked. If they liked dogs, he loved them but if they did not like canines, then he hated them. And so he would be like his targets in everything they did, liked or worried about.

Part one was to get them to like and admire him before he put them to the test by being nasty and threatening them that if they did not do what he wanted, then he would break the relationship off.

Of course, what he really wanted was obedience and the expression of their need for him so his narcissistic ego would grow and grow.

He was a perfectionist in many ways, but of course, a narcissist assumes that he is perfect anyway. The victims, the soul mates, had a duty to perceive him as he wanted to be seen or they would be removed from his life.

He needed to be liked for his swagger and charm, all of which had to be shone back at him or they would pay the price.

Fairly, rather really, was a technique he had picked up consciously or subconsciously, from his father. William had blamed his wife for his failings. He preferred drink to food and although mother was a good cook, and used fresh ingredients from the grocery shop, her husband decided that she was a bad chef. Likewise, he accused her of having affairs even though he told her she was too unattractive to find another man. Her lack of beauty was the reason he did not have sex rather than his impotence, he told her.

For Billy, women were fairly good looking because he would never choose an ugly partner so that they doubted their desirability for other men. They were sort of alright in bed but never that sexy. And so it went on. If, in their parallel universes, both were perfect then it did not match his needs. He had to be the best and had to be told as much by the less than perfect woman he was with.

A real relationship is a connexion between two people for the benefit of both. For Billy a liaison was nothing more than an opportunity for using somebody else for his own pleasure. To satisfy his narcissistic needs, he stood on the emotions of others. He would lead them into his idea of a relationship with promises by connecting to their needs.

It was as if he seduced a person to share a ride on a tandem and after a while, he would stop pedalling and enjoy the trip on the rear seat while the suffering front seat occupant did all the work.

For him it was a selling operation by finding the needs of people and fulfilling them and, if they did not know their own wants, then he would invent them for them.

He crept in to lives like a cancer. He was unseen as an destroyer and his targets felt no harm in the beginning but it then took over their lives and the only cure was to cut out the cause, but few knew that.

He made people feel guilty if they seemed to reject him. He wanted them to feel that they had made a mistake if they pushed him away by feeling that they were, in fact, pushing themselves away, not him. The flies that avoided the nectar of the Venus Fly

Trap were denying themselves the sweet rewards that were available. If they did not fall for him or showed signs of withdrawal then he threatened that they would be emotionally or even physically hurt.

His technique was straightforward but twisted and devious. To mix metaphors, he was a fisherman. He would bait his hooks and cast them into the water. He needed his victims to swim towards the bait, be pleased with what they found and then start to nibble. Then he would pull gently on the line to pull away a bit and the fish would chase the bait in case they lost it. Then he would wait until the lure was swallowed before pulling on the line to hook the target who could then not escape. When he landed the fish, he would unhook them and return them to the water if they did not fully fit his goals but he kept the unlucky ones.

His techniques were tried and tested. Drinks shared were as before with colleagues. Doubles for them and singles for himself and the need to match drinking rates. No date-rape drugs, just alcohol and his false charm.

He wanted his fish to give him respect, sympathy and to be vulnerable so they felt only Billy could sustain their lives. With the women he caught, he would build a sense of similarity. He would like what they liked after he found out more and more about them.

The objective was to create the sense that the women had found their dream lover, their soul mate who would be there for ever with a real love that they had never found before. They would help him to resolve his problems caused by others. He was a love-bomber and became a coercive controller when he needed to be the centre of everything. Everything he offered was conditional. 'If you really loved me, then…'

Like the fish, sometimes after he had unhooked them his plot would be discovered and the fish would swim away. He was convinced that he had gained when that happened. They had failed to see what a charming and wonderful person he was. Their loss, never his. 'Plenty more fish in the sea.' He would joke to himself as he planned his next angling trip.

Narcissists fall in love with themselves and look for others who will love them in the same way but they never can quite do that as well as him. When they do not seem to follow the rules then the threats start that they will lose the greatest love that had ever presented itself to them.

He would walk away and wait for the calls asking for his love again. The hook had become harder to disgorge. He would repeat what he had done to build that initial sense of love and reliance his victims had for him.

Part of what he did to diminish self-esteem was to remove support and love from others. Friends had to be pushed away and rejected. Family was dealt with in the same way after he had met them and shown what a great find their daughter, sister or niece had made. How could she be so silly as to reject him?

The process was the same as getting somebody addicted to drugs. The victim relied on them for what they saw as happiness and what was needed to survive in the hard and friendless world that they now lived in. Only Billy could save them. He was the supplier in return for them declaring love for Billy and putting up with his abuse.

He, of course was also a victim but he used this to his advantage. Previous partners and girlfriends made his life difficult with their mistrust. They always thought he was having affairs with other women, which he was but never admitted so. His mistrust grew from his deviousness and manipulation of the truth and he would accuse his girlfriends of having affairs when they were not. There was a double bluff. He had suffered because he had been falsely mistrusted and therefore needed the new women in his life to trust him to make him better.

The noose tightened bit by bit so that there would be a compulsion to please him in case he left for good.

The Venus Fly Trap was now closed and escape impossible. The hook was swallowed and embedded in the throat.

He had won. Then he became bored and his need to build his sense of beauty and self worth by finding new prey emerged. He was both a predator and a torturer. Once he had tempted his ladies into his spider's web of deception and illusion, he would push them into a hollow life without friends and relatives who would have helped them to escape before being totally consumed. He made threats that inhibited their getaway and tortured them with emotional hurt. Yet, now and again, his casualties would find freedom with the help of friends who, despite being ostracised, were still there because they saw what was happening. It would take time for the strands of silk to be loosened and the innocent captive could recognise her situation and act to find freedom from the emotional tyrant.

It never bothered him. It would be the time to move on. He wanted comfort and so he would research his potential targets. It was perfect if they were divorced and lived in a house without a mortgage. He would look at house values on the internet and he was as precise in his planning as an assassin in getting results without being caught out.

Part of his weakness that he never saw in himself was that in work, or with women, he expected loyalty although he was never loyal to anybody or anything. They were his toys that, like in his earlier life, he would destroy if he was unable to possess and own.

He felt that he was the Queen bee, or king in his mind. The drones would build the nest. He wanted to benefit from the steadfast work of others who were sacrificing their lives for the fulfilment of his joy.

A narcissist looks in the mirror lots and lots. He sees himself but in reverse, so he likes to take selfies to see himself the right way round. His problem is that he never sees himself as he really is. He is a person lost in a hall of mirrors. Some make him look short, others tall. Then fat, thin, distorted and so on. He is lost because he spends so much of his life looking for the one mirror that shows him as he knows he is; the perfect man. That makes him dependent upon the opinions of others who he trains to give the right answers for him.

He wanted the devotion that cult leaders had and based his relationships on hope and fear. His victims hoped he would change and improve their lives and their fear came from the feeling that he would not be as devoted to them as they were to him. Yet that was the impossible dream. He was only committed to himself.

21

They hoped that they could help him to become the original charmer that he was when they had met and the fear was that he would leave them if they could not.

THE ESCAPEES

There were potential victims of his controlling and abusive ways who escaped the spider's web; the jaws of the predator of emotions; the lure of deadly nectar in the plants that consumed those they attracted.

It always took time for the truth to show itself through the haze and fog of deception to expose the monster that was neatly disguised as the hero, the saviour, the soul mate.

The time taken would depend upon what was being done. It was always after weeks, months or years before the chrome wore off to expose the ugly rust hidden beneath the shiny surface.

Some friends of the victims who did not accept the sudden rejection of a buddy would find ways to penetrate the defences and talk to the casualties. Often pushed away because the friend was assumed to be jealous of such a perfect relationship, the trap was reinforced despite the inner emotional mind having doubts.

When self-belief is lost then there are only the beliefs of the narcissist to guide behaviour. The fly still consumes the nectar of the trap up until it starts to be eaten alive. Escape was not always an option but the women who broke out were not flies, they were people who could research, talk to others and build enough strength to stop their lives from being taken away by a parasite.

And that is what Billy was, a blood sucker who lived on his ill gotten gains from businesses, the innocent people who believed his insurance pitches as well as the women whose lives he stained, hopefully just in the short term before they rescued themselves or who were salvaged.

There was a price to pay, however. After a hunter attacks there are scars. Maybe bruises and marks. Perhaps financial problems. There are always emotional wounds, however, in every case that need to be healed, not with ointments or splints but by talking to trusted friends who will reassure the victim that they were not foolish, stupid, idiotic or weak minded but they were trapped by an expert in the manipulation of innocent people.

I wrote this from the bits and pieces I recalled from his

bragging as a young man before he left home and disappeared from my life. I spoke to some of his victims who I contacted after I took his keys for his grand apartment and by using his address book and phone while he was dying in the hospice. They were happy to tell me what he was like and what he did. After I told them that Billy was dying, they often spoke to me as if in a confessional as a way of cleaning the vile remnants of their user.

Others I had tried to contact had blocked any contact from him as a means of escape and so they were unaware of what was happening to the man who had polluted their lives.

One person I called, Shirley, filled me in with a lot of detail. She was reluctant to talk to me at first as the brother of the man who had damaged her but she returned my call after a few days and talked to me as if she was on the couch of a therapist.

I never met her but she had obviously been locked in a mental cell but with the news of Billy's coming demise, she opened up.

I will share her story in my words from what I remember of what she said.

I wish I had recorded her outpouring but that would have put pressure onto a victim who had been pressured enough into her submission.

His lies jumped out as he had tried to build his need for her to be sympathetic. One was about how the scar on his arm came from defending a girl who was being threatened by a man with a knife in a night club. He had fought him off even though he had been stabbed. The truth was, and I knew it, he had fallen off his bike while trying to do a wheelie and had cut himself on the handlebars.

Like most things in his life, he did his best to take advantage of others by inventing a new truth about himself.

Back to fishing. He threw ground bait into the water and then sat back until he was approached. He did this on dating apps, grooming his prey with sweet words, compliments, mirroring them until he was able to reel them in. This was how he had caught Shirley who had fallen for his lines, literally, and she was left craving the attention of the man who was, in her mind, her soul mate.

Her story was much longer than I have written down but I needed to avoid giving away too much detail of the methods he used to protect readers from the huntsmen who might want to use this as a training manual.

She described Billy as an emotional parasite who slowly took over by sucking her life out but leaving enough for the host to live on, albeit weakened and drained.

However, she eventually took control of her own life for herself when a hand written note was delivered to her house while Billy was away. It told her that her aunt had died and gave the details of the funeral. There was also a piece that said Julie, her cousin was worried that they had lost contact and that she neither answered her phone or replied to social media messages because she had been blocked.

Shirley had loved her aunt and felt guilty that she had not known about her passing. She took a deep breath and decided she would go to the funeral. When she told Billy he became extremely angry and accused her of arranging a meeting with a lover.

She showed him the note and told him when, where and with whom she would meet. He reluctantly agreed but while she was travelling, when she was at the funeral he messaged her continuously. Her cousin asked who this was who was constantly checking on her and Shirley avoided saying. She said that she was not going to the wake because she needed to get home. Then Julie took her to the side outside the church and told her about her ex-boyfriend who was a control freak. She had recognised the signs and, as if in simple conversation and with no questioning of Shirley, Julie said that with her lover, the constant calls when they were apart were to check on where she was and what she was doing and the need to confirm that she was not meeting up with other men.

The tale of woe she told fitted what had gone on with how Billy was, perfectly. Shirley burst into tears and explained what was happening to her. The threats, the accusations, the control and her fear of having contact with anybody other than Billy. She asked Julie how she had got away and realised that the very people who could help her were the ones who he had made her banish.

All the time, her phone pinged and after a while she stopped reading his messages and blocked him.

They both attended the wake and Julie followed her home in her car. When they both arrived at the door, Billy came storming out with his fists in the air. Shirley told him to pack his things and go. He at first refused, told her how much she would miss him and then went into a torrent of abuse. He even accused her of having a lesbian lover when he saw her cousin.

Julie stepped in, told Billy that she had videoed what was going on and told him that she would call the police if he did not go immediately. He swore at her and moved towards her aggressively just as her strong looking brother and his friend pulled up, got out of the car and told him to do what he had been instructed to do or they would 'hurt' him. That order was given in a very hostile way that gave Billy no choice. They waited until he had packed, loaded his car and got in to the driver's seat and had driven away.

The message that they would come back and sort him out if he tried to return was not spoken, but implied.

Billy went off to search for his next victim and Shirley never heard from him again. He had been blocked from her phone and from her life.

Real friends offer genuine love expecting nothing in return. False friends, the narcissists, the coercive controllers only offer hurt in exchange for their desperate need to be praised for nothing.

It took time before Shirley started to resume the life she had before Billy crept into her world and she spoke to her friends to explain what had happened. They were all sympathetic and understood. Some of them had heard about people like him before and offered more support for her.

THE TOMB

So I, the half-brother of a horrible man, am the author of this short exposé of that monster.

I am a normal man, happily married, blessed with grandchildren and a polar opposite of the man I went to see burnt in the crematorium. Luckily, Billy never had children who might have been moulded into the same vile shape as their father, but they would have presented competition for the love of the unfortunate mother who was made pregnant by a devil and that would have destroyed her.

I received a phone call telling that Billy was dying and was in a hospice. After many years of no contact, I visited him and found that I had no sympathy. As I said earlier, I took his keys from the drawer next to his bed and told him I would return with fresh clothes despite him never needing anything to wear apart from the gown he lived, and would have died, in.

In his home I discovered too many things that told his life in detail. The photographs of naked women in sexual poses, a large number of mobile phones but hidden away in a cupboard, I found his diary that showed so much, a lot of which I have put in this journal.

I was the only person at his cremation apart from the officials. Mother had died many years ago and Sally refused to even acknowledge that Billy was her brother, especially after he had refused to go to our mother's funeral because he was too busy.

I was there because I needed to see my brother's body destroyed in the hope that the dark memories of his victims would evaporate away in the smoke.

My eulogy was to tell anybody about Billy the bully. Then I hoped that there is an afterlife and he would hear what a horrible man he had been before entering hell.

The people he had hurt would not be there, but the memories of what had happened to his innocent prey would.

In the end everything I heard and remembered were like pieces of a jigsaw puzzle which I had to put together. The picture they made when completed was grotesque and scary. There again, Billy was as shallow as a piece of cardboard in the end, fit only to take apart, put in a bag and throw away which in a way, happened.

I am his brother and, even as he was dying, he liked to boast about how great he was how and he had achieved his goals and being without conscience about the people he had hurt. Yet those goals were hollow and as meaningful as the results from a soccer match the year before.

All those people in his life who were too nice to be glad he was dead can now be relieved that the scars they carried can now be healed.

We hear it said that so-and-so died peacefully and for Billy, unlike his victims, there was no physical pain. He suffered from the hallucinations and nightmares brought about by his mixture of painkillers and my hope was that the experiences of fear would be matched with how he made other people feel.

There was one, told to me by a nurse, where he watched young African women being filmed for a documentary. They walked into the desert and blood red plant spikes suddenly grew out of the sand, attached themselves to the first girl and dragged her down into a hole. The other women pulled her out and burnt her body. Then they scraped flakes off her skull that turned into little crab like creatures before running away and submerging themselves into the desert waiting for the next victim, their source of food. The camera man making the documentary just watched and filmed with no attempt to rescue the poor girl.

He had told the nurse the story of his nightmare with the fear still in his mind.

When I heard it, I laughed. He was the monster who consumed women and discarded the remains. Perhaps something in his mind, in his last hours, acknowledged what he had done to others.

After I laughed, the nurse lectured me on my lack of love and what a wonderful person Billy was. He had even used his last breaths to love bomb her. A dying viper's poison never diminishes even when it has no practical use for it. I choked on her words, laughed again and walked away for the last time.

Specifics about what was to be done with his body were never

28

discussed in great detail, but I was determined to keep my word but, in my way rather than his.

From that failed attempt to find nice things to say about him, I decided to outline his life in far more words under the working title of, 'From the Womb to the Tomb, the Horrible Life of a Nasty Controlling, Abusive, Narcissistic Power Freak.' That might change.

If you were one of his many victims, rejoice in his passing and the relief you will get from knowing he has gone for ever.

I will, I know.

He wanted attention even after he had died. I did my best to keep my promise that he would be interred in a tomb in a large plot after being taken away by a big hearse. My pledge was very tongue in cheek, however.

I wrote on his container the words from 'trash to ash, ash to trash' in indelible ink from a marker pen. I dropped it into a plastic sack and then into the dustbin.

He would have been taken away and dumped where people would not know where he was, but there again nobody needed to know because nobody would mourn him anyway. So his tomb was a plastic pot in a large plot under other rubbish in landfill having been delivered in a garbage truck as his hearse.

In a way that makes me as bad as he was but, there again, the revenge I sought was for a lot of people as well as for myself, mother and my sister and the hurt inflicted would not have been felt because he was dead after all, but the people he injured were alive at the time he was doing it.

Predators work under the cover of darkness where they stalk and catch their prey without being seen. Disguise and camouflage were important to him. Like a buzzard, he flew high and out of sight and then swooped to catch his victims. There was no remorse for him. It was a game of one winner and lots of losers. He made sure he always won but this time, his life had been taken away from him.

There is a punchline. As next of kin, all of his money came to

29

Sally and me and we decided to launder it in the true sense of the word. We made it clean. It went to charities for abused men and women as well as the homeless. Sally and I both knew he would have hated that.